SHATTERED RAINBOWS

J.L. GRACE

For more information, or to book an event, contact :

urbanheroes1@outlook.com

https://bit.ly/3yBHV5j

Book design by : AC Guzman

Cover design by : AC Guzman

ISBN - Paperback : 979-8-3302-0139-6

First Edition - May 2024

For Alex—

May your story inspire others to choose love over fear.

Prologue

The night everything changed was like any other. It was an ordinary Tuesday evening, the kind that slipped by unnoticed in the rhythm of everyday life. Yet, beneath the surface, the air crackled with an energy that felt like an impending storm. The dining room, once a place of warmth and laughter, had become a battleground for unspoken truths.

I watched my brother, Alex, sit at the head of the table, his hands trembling as he glanced nervously at our parents. His usual confidence had vanished, replaced by a palpable fear that tugged at my heart. Our parents sat on either side, their faces masks of neutrality, but the tension in their bodies betrayed the turmoil beneath.

The silence was suffocating, each tick of the clock amplifying the dread in the room. I found myself holding my breath, waiting for the moment when Alex would speak the words that had weighed heavily on his heart for so long. Finally, he cleared his throat, his voice barely a whisper.

That night, our family was irrevocably changed. The house, once filled with laughter and love, was now silent, echoing with the pain of unspoken words and shattered dreams. Little did we know, it was the beginning of a journey that would take us through the depths of despair and towards the light of acceptance.

This is Alex's story. This is my story. This is our story. A story of love, loss, and the enduring power of acceptance

.

"I'm... I'm gay."

For a moment, the world stopped. The words hung in the air, heavy and suffocating. My mother's gasp shattered the silence, followed by the clatter of silverware as my father's fork slipped from his fingers. Then, like a volcano, my father's anger erupted, unleashing a torrent of hurtful words that cut through the air like a knife.

"Faggot," he spat, his voice dripping with venom. "Queer. You're no son of mine."

Tears welled in my mother's eyes as she buried her face in her hands. I reached out to Alex, placing a comforting hand on his shoulder, but before I could offer solace, my father shoved me away with a force that sent me reeling.

Pain seared through my arm as I stumbled backward, my heart breaking at the sight of my brother, rejected and alone. In a moment that would haunt me forever, our parents pushed him out into the cold night, casting him aside like yesterday's news. From the upstairs window, I watched as he disappeared into the darkness, his backpack slung over his shoulder.

CONTENTS

Chapter 1

The Night Everything Changed

The dining room was charged with an energy that felt like an impending storm. It was a typical Tuesday evening, but the air was thick with anticipation, the weight of unspoken truths hanging over us like a dark cloud. My brother, Alex, sat at the head of the table, his hands trembling slightly as he stole nervous glances at our parents. His usual confidence had evaporated, replaced by a palpable apprehension that tugged at my heartstrings.

Our parents, seated on either side of him, maintained carefully neutral expressions, but the tension was evident in the tight set of my father's jaw and the rigidity in my mother's posture. They too sensed the impending revelation. My father's eyes were like ice, piercing and unyielding, while my mother's lips were pressed into a thin line, betraying her inner turmoil.

The minutes ticked by in agonizing silence. I found myself holding my breath, waiting for Alex to unburden his heart. The sound of the clock ticking seemed to grow louder, each second stretching into an eternity. Finally, Alex cleared his throat, his voice barely above a whisper as he spoke the words that would irrevocably alter our lives.

"I'm... I'm gay."

The words hung in the air, dense and suffocating. For a moment, time stood still as we all grappled with the enormity of his revelation. My mother's gasp shattered the silence, followed by the clatter of silverware as my father's fork slipped from his fingers, striking his plate with a dull thud. And then, like a volcano erupting, my father's anger exploded, unleashing a torrent of hurtful words that cut through the air like a knife.

"Faggot," he spat, his voice laced with venom. "Queer. You're no son of mine."

Tears welled in my mother's eyes as she buried her face in her hands, her sobs muffled by grief. I reached out to Alex, placing a comforting hand on his trembling shoulder, but before I could offer solace, my father's hand shot out, shoving me away with a force that sent me sprawling. Pain seared through my arm as I stumbled backward, my heart breaking at the sight of my brother, rejected and alone, his eyes a mix of fear and defiance.

In a moment that would haunt me forever, our parents pushed him out into the cold night, discarding him like yesterday's news. From the upstairs window, I watched as he disappeared into the darkness, his backpack slung over his shoulder as he hailed a taxi. As he drove off into the night, leaving behind shattered dreams and broken hearts, I mouthed, "Please don't go," knowing deep down that he could never truly stay.

The days that followed were a blur of anger, tears, and unanswered questions. Our family, once so close, was now fractured beyond repair. My father retreated into a sullen silence, refusing to speak of Alex, while my mother wandered the house like a ghost, her eyes red and swollen from crying. The atmosphere at home was stifling, a heavy blanket of grief and regret that threatened to smother us all.

I spent hours in Alex's room, surrounded by the remnants of his life. His posters, his books, his clothes—all served as painful reminders of what we had lost. I couldn't understand how my parents could be so cruel, how they could turn their backs on their own son. I was consumed by a burning anger, not just at them, but at myself for not doing more to protect him.

I replayed that night over and over in my mind, wondering if there was something I could have said or done to change the outcome. But the truth was, Alex had been struggling for a long time, and his coming out was just the final straw. The weight of our parents' expectations, the fear of rejection, the isolation— it had all become too much for him to bear.

As the weeks turned into months, the emptiness left by Alex's absence became a constant ache. I missed his laugh, his sense of humor, his unwavering support. I missed my brother. But more than that, I was haunted by the knowledge that he was out there somewhere, alone and hurting, because of the people who were supposed to love him the most.

Chapter 2

C h i l d h o o d   M e m o r i e s

In the days following that fateful night, as the wounds of our fractured family festered, I found solace in memories of our childhood, moments of innocence and joy now so distant. I remembered the magic of Christmas mornings, the excitement of waking to find presents piled high beneath the tree, and the thrill of meeting Santa Claus at the local mall. Alex would tug at my sleeve, eyes shining with wonder as he whispered his deepest wishes into Santa's ear, his smile a beacon of hope.

We were inseparable, Alex and I, joined at the hip from the moment we were born. We performed in school plays, our voices blending in harmony as we brought to life characters from distant lands and magical realms. We won talent shows and awards, our names immortalized on plaques and trophies adorning the walls of our childhood home.

But it wasn't just the big moments I cherished; it was the little things too. The late-night conversations under the covers, whispered secrets drifting through the darkness like fireflies. The birthday parties, sleepovers, and endless games of hide-and-seek.

Of course, there were fights, the inevitable clashes that come with sharing a life so closely entwined. We bickered and argued, traded insults and accusations, but through it all, our love for each other was fierce and unconditional, a bond that seemed unbreakable.

One Christmas stands out in my memory. We had just finished decorating the tree, its branches heavy with ornaments and twinkling lights. Alex and I sat on the floor, our backs against the couch, drinking hot chocolate and basking in the warmth of the fire.

He leaned his head on my shoulder and whispered, "Do you think Santa will bring me what I asked for?"

I smiled, knowing that he had asked for a new bike, something our parents couldn't afford. "I'm sure he will," I replied, wrapping an arm around him. "Santa always knows what we need."

That night, we stayed up late, talking about our hopes and dreams. Alex confided in me about his fears, his insecurities, and I did my best to reassure him. We fell asleep under the tree, the glow of the lights casting a soft halo around us.

Another cherished memory is of our summer vacations. Every year, we would go to the beach, spending lazy days building sandcastles, swimming in the ocean, and collecting seashells. Alex loved the water, and I can still see him now, diving into the waves with a carefree abandon that seemed to wash away all his worries.

We would sit on the shore, watching the sunset, and talk about the future. Alex always dreamed big—he wanted to travel the world, to experience everything life had to offer. He had such a zest for life, a curiosity that was infectious. He made me believe that anything was possible.

As I sifted through our childhood memories, each more precious than the last, I longed for the innocence of those days, the simple joy of being together, of being a family. Even as I mourned what we had lost, those memories remained a beacon of light in the darkness, a reminder of the love that once bound us and the hope that still lingered in my heart.

Chapter 3

T h e   U n s p o k e n   T r u t h

Looking back, I realize there were signs, subtle hints scattered like breadcrumbs leading to that fateful night. Small, seemingly insignificant moments that, in hindsight, took on profound significance. I remembered how Alex would linger in front of the mirror, obsessing over his hair and clothes. The posters of boy bands and heartthrobs on his walls, their smoldering gazes watching over us as we lounged on his bed, dreaming of futures beyond our small town.

Then there were the stolen glances and secret smiles, moments when our eyes would meet across a crowded room and something unspoken would pass between us, a silent understanding beyond words. Deep down, I always knew Alex was different, that he didn't fit into the neat little box society had assigned him. But I never dared speak the truth aloud, never confronted the reality lurking just beneath the surface.

One summer, Alex had a friend named Jake. They were inseparable, spending every waking moment together. I remember watching them, the way they would laugh and joke, the easy camaraderie between them. There was a closeness, an intimacy that I couldn't quite put my finger on.

One afternoon, I walked into Alex's room to find them sitting on his bed, their heads close together as they whispered. They pulled apart quickly, guilt flashing in their eyes. I brushed it off at the time, but now, looking back, I realize it was one of the many clues I had missed.

Another memory that stands out is of a family barbecue. Alex was quieter than usual, his eyes following one of our neighbors, a boy his age, with a look that I couldn't quite understand. It was a look of longing, of unspoken desire. I didn't question it then, but now it all makes sense.

As the pieces of the puzzle fell into place, I felt a wave of guilt. How could I have been so blind? How could I have missed the signs? But the truth was, Alex had been hiding his true self for so long, afraid of the consequences, afraid of losing the love and acceptance of his family.

We danced around each other, tiptoeing through a minefield of unspoken truths and hidden desires until that night when everything changed, when Alex found the courage to speak his truth and our world came crashing down. It was a truth that had been simmering beneath the surface, a truth that, once revealed, could never be taken back.

Chapter 4

T h e   L a s t   G o o d b y e

In the aftermath of that night, Alex's calls became fewer and far between. Each time, his voice sounded more distant, hollower, as if he was slipping away from us bit by bit. I tried to reach out, to bridge the gap that had grown between us, but my efforts felt like they were in vain.

One evening, the phone rang. It was Alex, his voice trembling with a mixture of resolve and resignation.

"I just wanted to say goodbye," he said, his voice barely a whisper. "I love you, but I can't do this anymore."

Panic surged through me. "Alex, please, don't do anything rash. Come home, we can work through this together."

But he had already hung up. I frantically called our parents, but by the time they reached his apartment, it was too late.

They found him hanging from the ceiling, a sign clutched in his hand that read, "I am sorry." The sight was too much for my mother, who collapsed in tears, while my father stood there, stunned and silent, his face pale and expressionless.

The days that followed were a haze of grief and disbelief. I couldn't comprehend the reality of what had happened, couldn't accept that Alex was gone. The pain was a constant, gnawing ache, a reminder of the hole that had been torn in my heart.

I found myself constantly replaying our last conversation, haunted by his words, by the despair in his voice. I felt a crushing guilt, a sense of failure that I hadn't been able to save him. I was angry at my parents, at the world, but mostly, I was angry at myself.

In the days leading up to his funeral, I found a letter in his apartment, addressed to me. "Dear Sister," it began, each word a dagger to my heart. "I'm sorry for the pain I've caused, for the burden I've placed on your shoulders."

Tears streamed down my face as I read his words, my heart aching with a grief too profound for words. "I love you," he wrote, his voice a whisper in the darkness, a final farewell to the sister he left behind.

Clutching his letter to my chest, I vowed to honor his memory, to live in a way that would make him proud, to never forget the brother I lost but to carry him with me always, in my heart and soul.

Chapter 5

Finding Purpose in Pain

As the numbness of grief faded and the pain of loss settled like a stone in my chest, I found a new purpose, a calling that whispered to me in the quiet of the night. I began volunteering at a halfway house for runaway teens, offering friendship to those cast aside by society, those who, like my brother, had been rejected simply for being who they were.

In the eyes of those lost souls, I found solace and strength, a flicker of hope amidst the darkness. Listening to their stories, filled with pain and longing, I realized I wasn't alone. There were others who shared my grief, my anger, my determination to make a difference.

Throwing myself into the work with passion and fervor, I guided those lost souls toward acceptance and self-discovery, offering them a glimmer of hope in a world determined to crush their spirits. The more I listened, the more I understood the profound impact of rejection, the deep wounds inflicted by those who were supposed to love unconditionally.

One evening, I met a boy named David. He reminded me so much of Alex—his smile, his spirit, his vulnerability. David had been kicked out of his home when his parents discovered he was gay. He had been living on the streets, struggling to survive, carrying the weight of his parents' rejection.

We sat together in the common room, and he shared his story with me. "I thought they would love me no matter what," he said, tears streaming down his face. "But they turned their backs on me. I don't understand how love can just disappear."

I reached out, taking his hand in mine. "David, it's not your fault. Their rejection doesn't define you.

You are worthy of love, just as you are."

In that moment, I saw a glimmer of hope in his eyes, a spark that had been dimmed by pain. It was a reminder of why I was there, why I had to keep fighting. For Alex, for David, for all the others who had been cast aside.

Chapter 6

Embracing Love and Acceptance

Surrounded by the echoes of the past and whispers of the future, I am reminded of a simple truth: love knows no bounds, and acceptance is the cornerstone of humanity. In a world plagued by prejudice and fear, it is our duty to embrace diversity and celebrate the rainbow of identities that make us who we are.

How does one being gay affect you? It doesn't. It shouldn't. We are all human, deserving of love and acceptance regardless of who we love or how we choose to live. Let us stand together, united in our quest for equality, for justice, for love. Let us honor the memory of those we've lost by fighting for a future where no one is judged or condemned for simply being who they are.

For in the end, love will always triumph over hate, and the light of acceptance will shine brightly, casting out the darkness. As I reflect on Alex's life, I am reminded of the joy he brought, the love he shared, the lives he touched. His memory is a beacon of hope, a reminder that we must continue to fight for a world where everyone is accepted for who they are.

I think of the parents who are just discovering that their child is gay, and I implore them to choose love, to choose acceptance. Your child is still the same person, still the same heart, still the same soul. Love them, support them, stand by them. Because the alternative is a world filled with pain and regret.

One evening, as I was leaving the halfway house, I noticed a mural on the wall, painted by the teens who lived there. It was a vibrant rainbow, with the words "Love is Love" written beneath it. It was a testament to their resilience, their strength, their hope for a better future.

I stood there, gazing at the mural, feeling a sense of peace wash over me. It was a reminder that love is indeed the most powerful force in the world, capable of healing even the deepest wounds.

Epilogue: A Call to Action

Closing this painful chapter, I am filled with purpose and determination, a resolve to never forget my brother but to carry his memory always in my heart and soul. He was more than my brother; he was my friend, my confidant, my ally in a world that seemed determined to tear us apart. Though he is gone, his spirit lives on in my work, in the lives I touch, in the hearts I heal.

I urge you, dear reader, to join me in the fight for equality, for justice, for love. We are all in this together, bound by a common humanity that transcends race, gender, sexuality, and creed. How does one being gay affect you? It doesn't. It shouldn't. For love is love, and love knows no boundaries.

As we move forward into an uncertain future, let us remember my brother's words, a beacon of hope in a world filled with darkness. In the end, love will save us, heal us, set us free. Let us embrace love in all its forms and together build a brighter, more inclusive world for generations to come.

About the Author

J.L. Grace, a passionate advocate for equality and acceptance. With a talent for capturing the raw emotions of life's most challenging moments, she brings to light the stories of those who have been marginalized and misunderstood. Her work is inspired by personal experiences and a commitment to fostering a more inclusive and compassionate world. J.L. Grace's writing not only entertains but also educates and inspires readers to embrace diversity and stand against prejudice.

When she is not writing, J.L. Grace volunteers at local shelters and organizations dedicated to supporting LGBTQ+ youth. She believes in the transformative power of love and acceptance, a theme that resonates strongly in all her books. J.L. Grace lives in Texas with her husband and their three dogs.

For more information or to book an event, visit https://bit.ly/3yBHV5j.

Acknowledgments

This book would not have been possible without the unwavering support and love of many incredible individuals. First and foremost, I want to thank my brother, Alex. Though you are no longer with us, your spirit continues to inspire and guide me every day. This book is dedicated to you, with all my love.

To my parents, thank you for your strength and for eventually finding your way to acceptance and love. It's a journey we've taken together, and I'm grateful for your efforts to understand and support me.

Lastly, to every reader who picks up this book, thank you for taking the time to read and engage with Alex's story. May it inspire you to lead with love and compassion in all your relationships.

www.ingramcontent.com/pod-product-compliance
Lightning Source LLC
Chambersburg PA
CBHW021329160726
47994CB00004B/1678